First published in Great Britain by HarperCollins Publishers Ltd in 2000

1 3 5 7 9 10 8 6 4 2
ISBN: 0 00 710029 9

Picture Lions is an imprint of the Children's Division, part of HarperCollins Publishers Ltd

The HarperCollins website address is: www.fireandwater.com

Manufactured in China

THE LOST
ACORNS

NICK BUTTERWORTH

Collins

An imprint of HarperCollinsPublishers

"Mmm! I do love the autumn," said
Percy the park keeper. Percy was
out looking for a good place to plant the
last of his spring bulbs.

"Over there, I think," said Percy.
"My daffodils and snowdrops will look
wonderful around that holly bush."

As Percy set to work, a robin flew by and landed next to him.
"Hello, Percy. What a lot of berries!"

"Yes," said Percy. "That means it's going to be a long, cold winter."
The robin fluffed up his feathers and flew off with a shiver.

ercy carried on with his work, but
then, he stopped and stared at the
ground. There was a strange trembling
in the earth around the holly bush.

Suddenly, soil burst into the air and one of Percy's bulbs popped out of the ground, balanced on a little pink nose!

"Mole," sighed Percy, "I thought we agreed. No molehills on the grass."

The mole blinked in the sudden daylight.

"Sorry, Percy," he snuffled. "I got lost."

Percy smiled.

"Well, try to dig more carefully in future!"

Percy replanted the bulb. He still had quite a few left and so he decided to plant them around a large oak tree. But as he knelt down to start digging, something hit him on the head. An acorn!

Percy looked up, but he couldn't see anything. Then, another acorn bounced off his cap. This time he heard giggling.

"Come on, then," said Percy. "Show yourself, you rascal!"

A squirrel's head popped out.

"Boo!" she said. "I surprised you didn't I Percy?"

"You certainly did," Percy laughed.

The squirrel scampered down the tree and picked up her acorns.

"What are you doing?" she asked.

"I'm planting my spring bulbs," said Percy.

"Oh," said the squirrel. "I thought you were burying nuts for the winter. I've buried lots and lots."

"It's a good job you have," said Percy. "It's going to be a long, cold winter."

"Well, then," said the squirrel, "I'd better go and bury these last few. I've got an extra special secret hiding place!"

Soon, Percy had finished.

"There!" he said, shaking the soil off his trowel. "Time for tea and buttered toast."

But poor Percy hadn't gone very far when he got a nasty shock. Somebody had been digging up his bulbs.

Percy bent down and picked one up. There were small tooth marks on it. "Someone's been trying to eat my bulbs!" said Percy. "Who would do that?"

Then, Percy heard something, or some*one*. And the someone was not very happy.

P
ercy peered out from behind a tree.
There was the squirrel. She was digging
up another of his bulbs. She sniffed at it and
took a bite. Then, she threw it away.

"What on earth are you doing?" said Percy.

"Oh, Percy," said the squirrel in a shaky voice, "I've looked everywhere. I can't find them . . ."

"There, there," said Percy. "Now tell me, what can't you find?"

"My acorns!" she wailed. "I hid them in a special secret hiding place and now I can't remember where it is!"

"Don't worry," said Percy. "I'll help you collect some more."

"But there aren't any more," she sobbed.

"Well, in that case," said Percy, "we'll just have to go on digging until…"

But before he could finish, Percy was interrupted by a strange rumbling noise.

Suddenly, the mole burst out of the ground in a shower of acorns.

"Oh dear," he blinked. "Lost again. Sorry."
But Percy just laughed.

"It looks like the mole has found somebody's extra special secret hiding place," he chuckled.

"Oh thank you, thank you!" said the squirrel. "Now I'd better hide them again. Somewhere really safe."

"Er…not just yet," said Percy. "Not until you've helped replant my bulbs! Then we'll all go back to my hut for tea and buttered toast. Or perhaps you'd prefer acorns?"

NICK BUTTERWORTH was born in North London in 1946 and grew up in a sweet shop in Essex. He now lives in Suffolk with his wife Annette. They have two grown-up children, Ben and Amanda.

The inspiration for the Percy the Park Keeper books came from Nick Butterworth's many walks through the local park with the family dog, Jake. The stories have sold nearly three million copies and are loved by children all around the world. Their popularity has led to the making of a stunning animated television series, now available on video from HIT Entertainment plc.

Read all the stories about Percy and his animal friends. . .

then enjoy the Percy activity books.

And don't forget you can now see Percy on video too!